CW01424798

READING ABOUT

Sea Animals

by Janet Allison Brown

Aladdin/Watts
London • Sydney

Contents

THE SHORE   PAGE 4
Starfish • Crabs • Shellfish • Lobster • Shore fish
Flat fish • Jellyfish • Turtle • Seal • Walrus

THE REEF   PAGE 12
Coral reef • Butterfly fish • Lion fish • Clown fish
Angel fish • Shoal • Octopus • Moray eel
Sea snake • Blue shark

THE OPEN SEA   PAGE 20
Penguins • Dolphins • Humpback whale
Whale family • Sail fish • Fangtooth fish

Can You Find? • Do You Know? • Index

© Aladdin Books Ltd 2000

Designed and produced by
Aladdin Books Ltd
28 Percy Street
London W1P 0LD

First published in
Great Britain in 2000 by
Franklin Watts
96 Leonard Street
London EC2A 4XD

ISBN 0 7496 3967 9

A catalogue record for this book is
available from the British Library.

Printed in UAE

All rights reserved

Editor
Jim Pipe

Literacy Consultant
Jackie Holderness
Oxford Brookes University
Westminster Institute of Education

Design
Flick Book Design and Graphics

Picture Research
Brian Hunter Smart

Meet the animals of the sea. Learn about the crabs, fish and seals that live on the seashore.

See the sharks, eels and other fish that live among the rocks of a reef.

Visit the whales and dolphins in the open sea, far from land.

Reef

Starfish

Crabs

Shellfish

What animals have you seen on the seashore?

This red starfish clings to the rocks. Crabs and other animals make their homes in a shell.

A lobster has big claws. Snap! It uses them to catch small fish.

Lobster

Shore fish

You can often see little fish near the beach. They look like the rocks around them.

Some fish are flat. They hide in the sand on the sea bed.

Flat fish

Watch out for jellyfish when you swim.

They are hard to see, but they can give you a nasty sting!

Jellyfish

This turtle lives in the sea. But it crawls up onto the beach to lay its eggs under the sand.

Turtle

How does it swim?

9

Seal

Can you see
its flippers?

Seals breathe air, like us. But they can stay underwater for a long time. Then they rest on the shore.

A walrus is like a seal. It digs for shellfish with its white tusks.

Walrus

What is this fish nibbling?
It is coral. Coral looks like
plants but it is made of tiny
animals. It grows on rocks
near the shore, called a reef.

Coral reef

Many fish live near the coral because there is lots to eat.

Fish do not breathe air like us. They stay underwater all day.

Can you guess how these fish got their names?

Butterfly fish

Clown fish

Lion fish

14

Angel fish

Shoal

A group of fish is a shoal.

An octopus likes to hide in the reef. It jumps out and grabs fish that swim past.

An octopus has eight legs. Would you like to have eight legs?

An octopus swims backward.
To move, it lifts its legs and
squirts out water!

Octopus

Other animals hide in the rocks, just like an octopus!

Moray eel

Eels and sea snakes have long, thin bodies that can hide in holes.

Sea snakes

18

Blue shark

Sharks do not need to hide. They can swim fast and have rows of sharp teeth to bite with – chomp!

19

Penguins are birds that live by the sea. They walk in a funny way on land. But they are very good swimmers.

Penguins

Dolphins are very friendly. They follow boats and sometimes play with people in the water.

Dolphins

Do you like to play in the waves?
Dolphins do. As they swim they
jump out of the
water to breathe!

Whales are like very big dolphins. This whale is diving down to look for food. It opens its mouth and scoops up lots of tiny sea animals.

Humpback whale

Baby whales stay close to their mother in the sea.

Whale family

Sail fish

This fish has a pointed nose and a fin like a sail! It lives in the open sea. Here the water can be very deep.

It is so dark at the bottom, animals may live here that no one has seen.

This fangtooth fish lives in the deepest parts of the ocean. Can you see its big teeth?

The water around it is black because light from the sun does not reach this far down.

Fangtooth fish

Can You Find?

Some sea animals have special parts on their bodies.

Can you find a sea animal that has one of these parts?

Fin

Claw

Arm

Read the answers on page 32.

Read the
answers on
page 32.

Tail

Flipper

Clue: Look at pages
4, 5, 9, 12 and 23.

Clue: Look at pages
4, 5, 9, 12 and 23.

Do You Know?

Sperm whale

Sea animals swim in many ways. A whale pushes its tail up and down. A fish wiggles its body from side to side.

Dog fish

Crab

Do you know how a crab moves across the sea bed?

This seahorse wiggles its fins to move. Can you see what it uses its tail for?

The answers are on page 32.

Seahorse

Index

Angel fish 14
Arm 28

Blue shark 19
Butterfly fish 14

Claw 28
Clown fish 14
Coral reef 13
Crab 4, 31

Dog fish 30
Dolphin 22

Fangtooth fish
  27
Fin 28

Flat fish 6
Flipper 29

Humpback
  whale 24

Jellyfish 7

Lion fish 14
Lobster 5

Moray eel
  18

Octopus 17

Penguin 20

Reef 3

Sail fish 26
Seahorse 31
Seal 10
Sea snake 18
Shellfish 4
Shoal 15
Shore fish 6
Sperm whale 30
Starfish 4

Tail 29
Turtle 9

Walrus 11
Whale family 25

ANSWERS TO QUESTIONS

Page 28-29 – A dolphin has this **fin** • A lobster has this **claw** • A starfish has this **arm** • A fish has this **tail** • A turtle has this **flipper**.

Page 31– A **crab** crawls along the sea bed, moving sideways • A **seahorse** uses its tail to grab onto rocks on the sea bed.

Photocredits: Abbreviations: t-top, m-middle, b-bottom, r-right, l-left. Cover, 3, 8-9, 10, 11, 15, 16-17, 18, 20, 22, 24, 28m, 29m, 31r – Digital Stock. 1, 2ml, 2lt – John Foxx Images. 2mr, 4, 12-13, 19, 28br, 29t – Stockbyte. 6 – B.Borrell/FLPA. 7 – C.Marshall/FLPA. 27 – Bruce Robinson/Corbis. 31t – Select Pictures.
Illustrators: Dave Burroughs; Wayne Ford – Wildlife Art Ltd; Justine Peek, Norman Weaver.